THE FARMYARD JAMBOREE

For Richard Scholtz; I dance every time he plays! — M. R. M.
To my friend Serge — S. F.

Barefoot Books
294 Banbury Road
Oxford, OX2 7ED

Barefoot Books
2067 Massachusetts Ave
Cambridge, MA 02140

Text copyright © 2005 by Margaret Read Macdonald
Illustrations copyright © 2005 by Sophie Fatus
The moral rights of Margaret Read Macdonald and Sophie Fatus have been asserted
Sung by Bob King. Musical composition and arrangement © 2005 by Bob King
Recorded, mixed and mastered at Touchwood Studios, Regina, Saskatchewan, Canada
Animation by Karrot Animation, London

First published in Great Britain by Barefoot Books, Ltd and in
the United States of America by Barefoot Books, Inc in 2005
This paperback edition published in 2012
First published as *A Hen, a Chick and a String Guitar*

Graphic design by Judy Linard, London
Reproduction by B & P International, Hong Kong
Printed in China on 100% acid-free paper
This book was typeset in Bembo Schoolbook and Cerigo Bold
The illustrations were prepared in acrylics and pastels

ISBN 978-1-84686-718-7

British Cataloguing-in-Publication Data:
a catalogue record for this book is available from the British Library

Library of Congress Cataloging-in-Publication Data is available under
LCCN 2004017830

3 5 7 9 8 6 4 2

THE FARMYARD JAMBOREE

Inspired by a Chilean folktale

Written by
Margaret Read MacDonald

Illustrated by
Sophie Fatus

Sung by
Bob King

Barefoot Books
step inside a story

Grandpa gave me a clucking red hen.

"Cluck! Cluck! Cluck! Cluck! Cluck!"

Ay! Ay! Ay! What a fine hen!
"Cluck! Cluck! Cluck! Cluck! Cluck!"
One day that hen
Gave me a chick.
I had a hen,
And I had a chick.

Ay! Ay! Ay! Ay! Ay!
How I loved my two little pets!

Grandma gave me a quacking white duck.

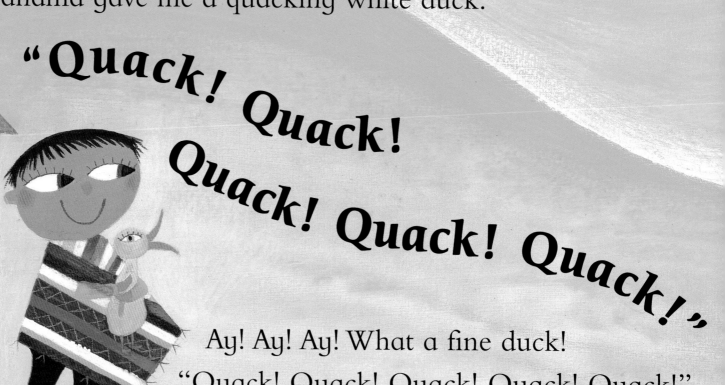

"**Quack! Quack! Quack! Quack! Quack!**"

Ay! Ay! Ay! What a fine duck!
"Quack! Quack! Quack! Quack! Quack!"
One day that duck
Gave me a duckling.

I had a duck,
And I had a duckling.
I had a hen,
I had a chick.

Ay! Ay! Ay! Ay! Ay!
How I loved my four little pets!

Uncle gave me a purring yellow cat.

"Purr! Purr! Purr!"

Ay! Ay! Ay! What a fine cat!
"Purr! Purr! Purr!"
One day that cat
Gave me a kitten.

I had a cat,
And I had a kitten.
I had a duck.
I had a duckling.
I had a hen.
I had a chick.

Ay! Ay! Ay! Ay! Ay!
How I loved my six little pets!

Auntie gave me a barking black dog.

"Woof! Woof! Woof! Woof! Woof!"

Ay! Ay! Ay! What a fine dog!
"Woof! Woof! Woof! Woof! Woof!"

One day that dog
Gave me a puppy.

I had a dog,
And I had a puppy.
I had a cat.
I had a kitten.
I had a duck.
I had a duckling.
I had a hen.
I had a chick.

Ay! Ay! Ay! Ay! Ay!
How I loved my eight little pets!

Brother gave me a bleating white sheep.

"Baa! Baa! Baa!"

Ay! Ay! Ay! What a fine sheep!
"Baa! Baa! Baa!"

One day that sheep
Gave me a lamb.

I had a sheep,
And I had a lamb.
A dog…a puppy.
A cat…a kitten.
A duck…a duckling.
A hen…a chick.

Ay! Ay! Ay! Ay! Ay!
How I loved my
ten little pets!

Sister gave me an oinking pink pig.

"Oink! Oink! Oink! Oink! Oink!"

Ay! Ay! Ay! What a fine pig!
"Oink! Oink! Oink! Oink! Oink!"
One day that pig
Gave me a piglet.

I had a pig,
And I had a piglet.
A sheep…a lamb.
A dog…a puppy.
A cat…a kitten.
A duck…a duckling.
I had a hen.
I had a chick.

Ay! Ay! Ay! Ay! Ay!
How I loved my twelve little pets!

Mother gave me a mooing brown cow.

"Moo! Moo! Moo!"

Ay! Ay! Ay! What a fine cow!
"Moo! Moo! Moo!"
One day that cow
Gave me a calf.

I had a cow,
And I had a calf.
A pig…a piglet.
A sheep…a lamb.
A dog…a puppy.
A cat…a kitten.
A duck…a duckling.
A hen…a chick.

Ay! Ay! Ay! Ay! Ay!
How I loved my fourteen pets!

Father gave me a neighing grey horse.

"Neigh! Neigh! Neigh!"

Ay! Ay! Ay! What a fine horse!
"Neigh! Neigh! Neigh!"
One day that horse
Gave me a colt.

I had a horse,
And I had a colt.

A cow…a calf!

A pig…a piglet!

A sheep…a lamb!

A dog…a puppy!

A cat…a kitten!

A duck…a duckling!

I had a hen,
And I had a chick.

Ay! Ay! Ay! Ay! Ay!
How I loved my sixteen pets!

My friend gave me a little guitar!

"Plunk! Plunk!

Plunk! Plunk! Plunk!

Ay! Ay! Ay! What a fine guitar!

"Plunk! Plunk! Plunk! Plunk! Plunk!"

And every time I played my guitar
My pets all came from near and far...

The horse danced
And the colt danced!

The cow danced
And the calf danced!

The pig danced
And the piglet danced!

The sheep danced
And the lamb danced!

The dog danced
And the puppy danced!

The cat danced
And the kitten danced!

The duck danced
And the duckling danced!

The hen danced
And the chick danced!

They all danced
And I danced too!

Ay! Ay! Ay! Ay! Ay!
How I love all of my pets!

SOURCES

This story was inspired by *Folklore Chileno* by Oreste Plath (Santiago: Nascimento, 1969). A similar text is found in *Folklore Portorriqueño* by Rafael Ramirez de Arellano (Madrid: Centro de Estudios Históricos, 1926). The tale appears as a folk song in *Folktales of Mexico* by Americo Paredes (University of Chicago Press, 1970). Chilean storyteller Carlos Genovese informs me that versions of this tale are told throughout Chile and Latin America. Usually the child has a "real y media" coin and begins buying animals. For this picture book, liberties have been taken with the tale to create a playful children's version in English. The Chilean version gave no music, so the musicians created the song on the accompanying disc. The tale seems to appear as a folk song in some areas and as a simple told story in others. The artist has chosen to illustrate the story with an Andean setting. The Aymara live in the north-easternmost corner of Chile.

For a guitar score to accompany this book,
please visit our website.